WITHDRAWN

Dear Parents and Educators,

Welcome to Penguin Young Readers! As parents and educators, you know that each child develops at his or her own pace—in terms of speech, critical thinking, and, of course, reading. Penguin Young Readers recognizes this fact. As a result, each Penguin Young Readers book is assigned a traditional easy-to-read level (1–4) as well as a Guided Reading Level (A–P). Both of these systems will help you choose the right book for your child. Please refer to the back of each book for specific leveling information. Penguin Young Readers features esteemed authors and illustrators, stories about favorite characters, fascinating nonfiction, and more!

The Hive: Babee's Room

LEVEL 2

GUIDED READING LEVEL **H**

This book is perfect for a **Progressing Reader** who:
- can figure out unknown words by using picture and context clues;
- can recognize beginning, middle, and ending sounds;
- can make and confirm predictions about what will happen in the text; and
- can distinguish between fiction and nonfiction.

Here are some **activities** you can do during and after reading this book:
- Sight Words: Sight words are frequently used words that readers know just by looking at them. These words are not "sounded out" or "decoded"; rather, they are known instantly, on sight. As you are reading or rereading the story, have the child point out the below sight words.

ask	going	thank
fly	just	want

- Make Connections: In this story, Rubee and Buzzbee are getting ready to welcome home a new baby. Have you ever waited for a new baby to come home? If you have not, imagine what it would be like. Write a paragraph about how you would get ready for a new baby.

Remember, sharing the love of reading with a child is the best gift you can give!

—Bonnie Bader, EdM
Penguin Young Readers program

*Penguin Young Readers are leveled by independent reviewers applying the standards developed by Irene Fountas and Gay Su Pinnell in *Matching Books to Readers: Using Leveled Books in Guided Reading*, Heinemann, 1999.

PENGUIN YOUNG READERS
Published by the Penguin Group
Penguin Group (USA) LLC, 375 Hudson Street, New York, New York 10014, USA

USA | Canada | UK | Ireland | Australia | New Zealand | India | South Africa | China

penguin.com
A Penguin Random House Company

Published in 2015 by Penguin Young Readers, an imprint of Penguin Group (USA) LLC, 345 Hudson Street, New York, New York 10014.
Manufactured in China.

ISBN 978-0-448-48227-9   10 9 8 7 6 5 4 3 2 1

Babee's Room

based on the episode by Bridget Hurst

Penguin Young Readers
An Imprint of Penguin Group (USA) LLC

"Good morning, little bees," says

Grandma Bee.

"Morning," says Buzzbee.

"Where are Mamma and
Pappa?" asks Rubee.
"They are bringing home a
brand-new baby," says Grandma.

"He will be very good at flying.

Just like me," Buzzbee says.

"No. *She* will be really good at painting, just like me," Rubee says.

The bees fly to their rooms.
They want to make their rooms
nice for Babee.

"Babee is going to share
my room!" Buzzbee says.
"We'll see about that!" Rubee
says.

Rubee draws pictures.

Buzzbee makes a mobile.

Rubee peeks into Buzzbee's room.

"Why didn't I think of that?"

she asks.

So she makes a mobile, too.

Buzzbee looks into Rubee's room.

"Why didn't I think of that?"

he asks.

And he draws pictures, too!

Buzzbee and Rubee practice

what they will say to Babee.

"Welcome home, Babee.

It is nice to meet you.

We can fly together.

I will be your favorite brother!"

Buzzbee says.

"Welcome home, Babee.

It is nice to meet you.

We can dance together.

I will be your favorite sister!"

Rubee says.

Ding-dong!

Babee is home!

"Look what I made for Babee,"
Rubee tells Mamma and Pappa.

"Babee should share my room."

23

"Look what I made for Babee,"
Buzzbee tells Mamma and Pappa.
"Babee should share my room."

"Your rooms are both nice," Mamma says.

"But Babee is not big enough to share a room with either of you."

Buzzbee and Rubee are sad.

"But Babee can visit your rooms," Mamma says.

Buzzbee and Rubee are happy about that.

Grandma brings in a box of diapers!

"Would you two like to change Babee's diaper?"

Mamma asks Buzzbee and Rubee.

"Ew, no thanks!"

Buzzbee and Rubee giggle.

Welcome home, Babee!